BEGINNER READER

The Fairyland Costume Ball

Orchard Beginner Readers are specially created to develop
literacy skills, confidence and a love of reading.

ORCHARD BOOKS

First published in Great Britain in 2016 by The Watts Publishing Group

1 3 5 7 9 10 8 6 4 2

© 2016 Rainbow Magic Limited.
© 2016 HIT Entertainment Limited.
Illustrations on p3 © Georgie Ripper
All other illustrations © Orchard Books 2016

HiT entertainment

A CIP catalogue record for this book is available from the British Library.

ISBN 978 1 40833 974 9

Printed in Great China

The paper and board used in this book are made from wood from responsible sources

Orchard Books
An imprint of Hachette Children's Group
Part of The Watts Publishing Group Limited
Carmelite House, 50 Victoria Embankment, London EC4Y 0DZ

An Hachette UK Company
www.hachette.co.uk
www.hachettechildrens.co.uk

Emily the Emerald Fairy

Amy the Amethyst Fairy

Chloe the Topaz Fairy

Meet the Jewel Fairies

The Jewel Fairies have some very special magic for you. It's time to join them on an adventure!

Lucy the Diamond Fairy

Scarlett the Garnet Fairy

Sophie the Sapphire Fairy

India the Moonstone Fairy

Red leaves drop from the trees.
It is autumn in Fairyland.

Halloween will be here soon.
The Jewel Fairies are excited.

Halloween is a magical time in Fairyland. The fairy king and queen always throw a grand costume ball.

All the fairies dress up, dance and celebrate. The Jewel Fairies want their costumes to be extra special.

Flora the Fancy Dress Fairy and Trixie the Halloween Fairy arrive at the Jewel Fairies' cottage.

They want to help their friends get ready for the ball.

"Halloween is fun because you can dress up however you want!" says Trixie.

"Let's all look for costumes that match the colour of our jewels," Sophie the Sapphire Fairy suggests.
"What a colourful idea!" Chloe agrees.

Amy the Amethyst Fairy searches through racks of dresses and stacks of masks, but she doesn't find anything special.

"What's wrong, Amy?" asks Trixie.
"I can't find the right costume for the ball,"
she explains.

"Do you want to look fancy? Silly? Scary?"
Trixie asks.

"I don't know," Amy admits. "I want to
surprise everyone."
"Hmmm." Trixie sighs. "We'll think of
something."

Finally, it's Halloween night.
The Jewel Fairies chat and laugh as
they get ready.

Scarlett the Garnet Fairy puts on her tiara.
Sophie paints whiskers on Chloe.

Lucy the Diamond Fairy puts on a snowy
headband.
"You look delicious!" India the Moonstone
Fairy tells Emily the Emerald Fairy.

Amy is in the corner with Trixie.
"What are you up to?" Chloe asks.

"Trixie is helping me put the last touches on
my costume," Amy says with a sly smile.
"What costume?" asks Scarlett.
"You'll see," Amy replies.

Finally, it is time to leave.
"Has anyone seen Amy?" India asks.

"It's like she disappeared," Emily says.
"She told me that she will meet you at the
ball," Trixie explains.

With hats, crowns, masks and make-up,
the fairies set out for the costume ball.

"Let's take a shortcut through the Enchanted
Forest," says Sophie. "It's faster."
"And spookier," Scarlett adds.

The shadows are long and dark in the forest.
A low moan echoes through the trees.

Scarlett shivers. "What was that?" she asks.
"I'm sure it was just the wind," Emily says, but
her voice trembles.

The fairies look around.
They don't see anyone.
They hear the low moan again.

OOOOOOOO, OOOOOOOOO

"It sounds like a ghost!" Lucy cries. She grabs India's hand.

The fairies feel a chill as the air rushes around them.

"I'm worried about Amy," Sophie says.
"She will be all alone."

At last, the Jewel Fairies reach the
Fairyland Palace.
It twinkles in the moonlight.
"It looks beautiful!" says Chloe.

"Let's hurry," Lucy says. "The ball is about to begin."

When they enter the palace, Queen Titania spots the Jewel Fairies.
"Welcome," she says. "But where is Amy?"

Just then, they hear the low moan again.

OOOOOOOO, OOOOOOOOOOO

A burst of purple sparkles appears.
"Boo! I'm a ghost!"

The Jewel Fairies shriek with surprise.
They know that voice.
It's Amy!

"You scared us!" Scarlett declares.
"You really didn't know it was me?" Amy asks.
"Not at all. That's a terrific costume," Flora tells Amy.

"I made it myself," Amy says, "with a little magic, of course!"
"Now we're all here! Let's have some Halloween fun," India says.

The Jewel Fairies join in the festivities.

Emily and Scarlett bob for apples.

Amy and Chloe eat pumpkin cupcakes.

All the fairies dance together.

At midnight, it's time for a special toast.
The Jewel Fairies raise their glasses.
"Happy Halloween!" announce the king
and queen.

Amy clinks her glass with Scarlett's. "Here's to
another magical year filled with surprises!"